This book is dedicated to kind and courageous children everywhere.

A Note for Parents and Teachers:

*Like all **Short Vowel Adventures**,* Rat Attack *highlights one short vowel sound, in this case the short "a" sound. We believe this phonics focus helps beginning readers gain skill and confidence. After the story, we've included two **Story Starters**, just for fun. **Story Starters** are open-ended questions that can be used as a jumping-off place for conversation, storytelling, and imaginative writing.*

At BraveMouse Books we believe the most important part of any reading program is the shared experience of a good story. We hope you'll enjoy Rat Attack *with a child you love!*

The BraveMouse Team

Copyright ©2014 Molly Coxe BraveMouse Books First Edition isbn 9781940947211

Rat Attack

by Molly Coxe

BraveMouse Readers

Brave Mouse Books

Gram is making jam
for Ann, Fran, and Stan.

She hears a tap.

"Who's that?" asks Gram.

"I'm a bandit, ma'am.
Hand over the jam!"

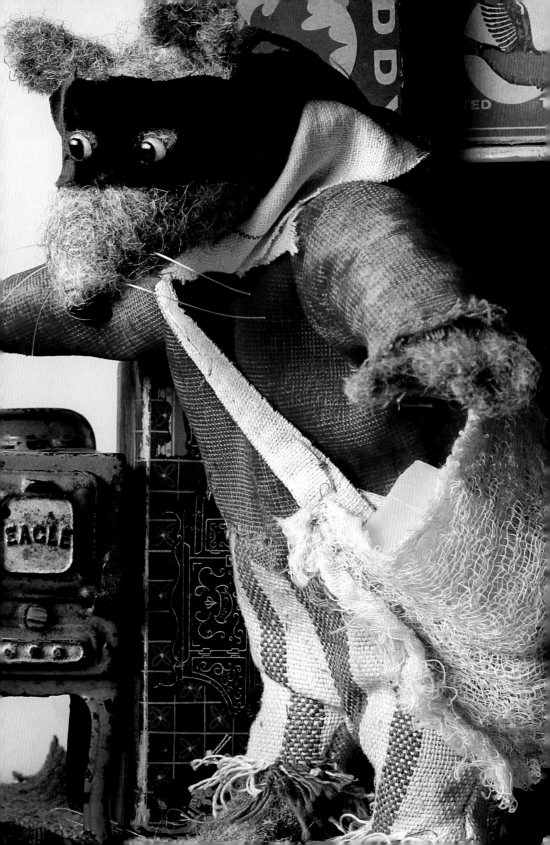

"You are not a bandit,"
says Gram.
"You are Nat, the rat.
Scat, Nat!"

Gram is making jam.
She hears a tap.
"Who's that?" asks Gram.

"I'm a monster!
Fee fi fo fum!
Give me jam
to fill my tum!"

"You are not a monster,"
says Gram.
"You are Pat, the rat.
Scat, Pat!"

Gram is making jam.
She hears a tap.
"Who's that?" asks Gram.

"I am a magician!
Put some jam in here.
I will make it disappear!"

"You are not a magician,"
says Gram.
You are Matt, the rat.
Scat, Matt!"

Gram is making jam.
She hears a tap.
"Who's that?" asks Gram.

"This is a rat attack!"
say Nat, Pat, and Matt.

"Ann, Fran, Stan, come fast!"
says Gram.

"The rats are stealing the jam!"
says Gram.

"We have a plan!"
say Ann, Fran, and Stan.

The rats hear a tap.
"Who's that?" ask the rats.

"This is a cat attack!"
say Ann, Fran, and Stan.

The rats scat.

"Anyone for jam?" says Gram.

"Yes, ma'am!"

say Ann, Stan, and Fran.

The End

Want to tell a story? Turn the page!

Story Starters

Ann has a plan.

What is Ann's plan?

The ladder goes up, up, up.
What will Ann find
at the top?